KU-443-274

THE Hans and Matilda SHOW

To Kodai and Gen

A TEMPLAR BOOK

First published in the UK in 2014 by Templar Publishing,
an imprint of The Templar Company Limited,
Deepdene Lodge, Deepdene Avenue,
Dorking, Surrey, RH5 4AT, UK
www.templarco.co.uk

Copyright © 2014 by Yokococo

First edition

All rights reserved

ISBN 978-1-84877-242-7 (hardback)
ISBN 978-1-84877-176-5 (paperback)

Edited by Hannah Pang

Printed in Malaysia

THE Hans and Matilda SHOW

templar publishing

There was once a little cat called Hans.

Everyone said that Hans was *so* naughty.

And there was once a little cat called Matilda.

Everyone said that Matilda was *so* good.

BUT…

Matilda had a secret

and a secret bag.

More about that later…

One day there was a talent show at school.

As the show started, everyone lined up.

NICE COSTUMES!

"Oh no! It's Clumsy Tony!"

said someone in the audience.

"Where is Hans?" said someone else.

The first performer was Matilda
doing her ballet dancing. She gracefully
twirled and fluttered across the stage.
The audience went wild!

After Matilda had finished
her performance,
she went backstage…

and got her SECRET BAG!

Inside her secret bag,

there was a coat

and a pair of boots.

And

a

scarf.

And
a
hat.

And
a
mask.

And...

... whiskers!

Yes, Hans was Matilda. And Matilda was Hans.

"I bet I can make the show a bit more exciting," said Hans.

The next performance

was a duet from The Beautiful Twins.

Their harmony was excellent,

but Hans thought their act needed

spicing up…

So Hans scattered pepper on them.

The poor twins! They couldn't stop sneezing.

Next it was Handsome Ben's turn.

He was such an amazing juggler!

But Hans had wanted to make the act really smashing…

So had swapped the juggling balls for eggs!

Then came the cancan dancers!

They were so pretty.

The audience was very impressed.

But Hans thought they needed

to make a bigger splash…

So he tipped a bucket of water over them!

Backstage, the performers were all very angry.

"We need to catch that naughty Hans!" they said.

"Look! There he is!" one of the dancers shouted.

"Come here, Hans!" the twins cried.

"After him,"

cried everyone.

Hans ran onto the stage just as Clumsy Tony

was asking for a volunteer to help

with his magic trick.

"Here I am!" said Hans,

bowing to the audience.

Clumsy Tony got

a volunteer much quicker than he thought!

"Goodbye, everyone!" said Hans.

"You can't escape now," cried everyone.

Clumsy Tony tapped the box
and said the magic words:

"3...2...1..."

Ta-da! Hans had totally disappeared
and in his place stood…
Matilda!

BRAVO!

It was **magic!**

The audience clapped and cheered...

WHAT A TRICK!

Clumsy Tony got the golden

medal for best talent act

in the show.

Everyone applauded.

And Hans and Matilda

had done so well…

… that they both
receieved silver
medals.

"But where is Hans?"
asked Clumsy Tony.

"Don't worry, I'll give him his medal," said Matilda.

And, of course, she did!